Dorothy and the Great Quake

A Story about Dorothy Day as a Young Girl

Written by Barbara Allaire and Illustrated by Vicki Shuck

Dedicated to Mary Farrell,
a Catholic Worker who invited me and my husband
to join her in starting a Catholic Worker house in 1991,
beginning our journey of fascination
with the life, vision, and work of Dorothy Day.
—B. A.

In memory of my mother, Joanna—
she would have loved this!
—V. S.

Dorothy Day and her little sister, Della, had just finished doing chores for their mother. Now they had a few hours to play in the April sunshine before dinner.

"Let's find Naomi," Dorothy suggested, "and go to the hiding place!"

The hiding place was a secret spot the girls had found among some lilac bushes. Once they wriggled their way inside, it was like a little room in there, with leaves for walls and a roof. And now the lilacs were in bloom, and they smelled like Mama's perfume.

"Can I bring my Annabelle?" Della asked. Annabelle was her doll.

"Of course!" Dorothy said. "And I'll bring Rebecca."

3

The sisters found Naomi sitting on the stoop of her mother's tiny grocery store eating a cracker.

"Hi there, Naomi," Dorothy called. "Do you want to come to the hiding place with us? There are so many pretty purple flowers there, and we're going to make flower chains for our dolls. Only, we have to sneak so the boys don't see us."

It would be a disaster if Dorothy's older brothers discovered their secret place!

But Naomi looked solemn. "Mama says I can't play with you anymore," she said slowly.

"Why not?" Dorothy asked.

Naomi looked down at her lap. "Because you're too rough, and you fight with your brothers. And—your father goes to horse races!"

Dorothy's face flushed hot. "I am not too rough!"

"Yes, you are! You fought with Donald yesterday, and you called him—that bad name! My mama heard you."

Dorothy remembered, and she was embarrassed that Mrs. Reed had heard her. Mrs. Reed was a respectable, churchgoing woman. She had even let Dorothy borrow her second-best Bible. And now she thought Dorothy was *bad*.

"But he stole Rebecca, and he wouldn't give her back!" Dorothy protested, hugging her doll closer.

"Naomi!" Mrs. Reed called from inside the store. "I need your help."

"Sorry," Naomi said sadly to Dorothy.

Dorothy stood very still, trying not to cry.

"Come on, Della," she said at last. "We don't need Naomi to have fun."

But in her heart, Dorothy didn't believe her own words. She did need her friend.

"Don't worry, Dorothy—I'll be your bestest friend!" Della declared, taking Dorothy's hand.

Dorothy laughed, and the two sisters hugged. Dorothy remembered what her mama always said: "When you're feeling low, try to be cheerful." How could she not be cheerful with such a good sister?

"Let's walk to the pharmacy," Dorothy suggested. "Maybe Mr. Gerber will give us a penny candy."

7

By dinnertime, Dorothy felt a little better. Mama always made home feel good. She had set the table with her lovely china dishes and placed a vase of springtime flowers in the middle. Light from the chandelier danced on the silverware, and the food smelled so good!

"Let's have good manners, children," Mama said. She gave Dorothy's loud, squirmy brothers a stern look to make them behave. "Papa's had a long day."

Papa always had a long day, because he worked as a sports reporter for a newspaper across the bay in San Francisco. Dorothy enjoyed hearing the stories he told Mama about what was happening in the big city.

"Well, children," Mama said as they passed around the serving dishes, "did anything interesting happen today?"

Della piped up right away. "Naomi can't be friends with Dorothy anymore, because Mrs. Reed says she's too rough."

"Oh, Dorothy!" Mama exclaimed sadly. She shook her head.

"Naomi also said Papa went to horse races," Della went on. "Is that bad?"

"It's not bad!" said Dorothy. "It's his job to write about the races."

"I wouldn't pay much mind to the opinion of the neighbors, Dorothy," Papa said. "If they don't want to be friendly, then so be it."

But Dorothy couldn't help minding.

At bedtime, Dorothy read
Della one of the scribbles
Dorothy liked to write
in a little, pink notebook.
This one was a story about
the adventures of two sisters
who took a train to India.

That night,
Dorothy dreamed
of a train with
a loud, roaring
engine. The train
got louder and
louder until . . .

. . . it woke Dorothy up, rolling her brass bed back and forth across the polished floor. The books tumbled off their shelves, and the lamp fell to the floor with a crash. She heard things falling and breaking all over the house. Dorothy covered her ears to make that horrible roaring stop!

When at last it was quiet, Dorothy carefully crept out of bed. Where were Mama and Papa? Where were Della and Donald and Sam? Dorothy searched through the house.

The dining room that
had been so warm and
cozy last night was a mess.
All the pretty china dishes
lay in pieces on the floor,
food had spilled from
the cupboards, and the
chandelier was smashed
into a million bits.

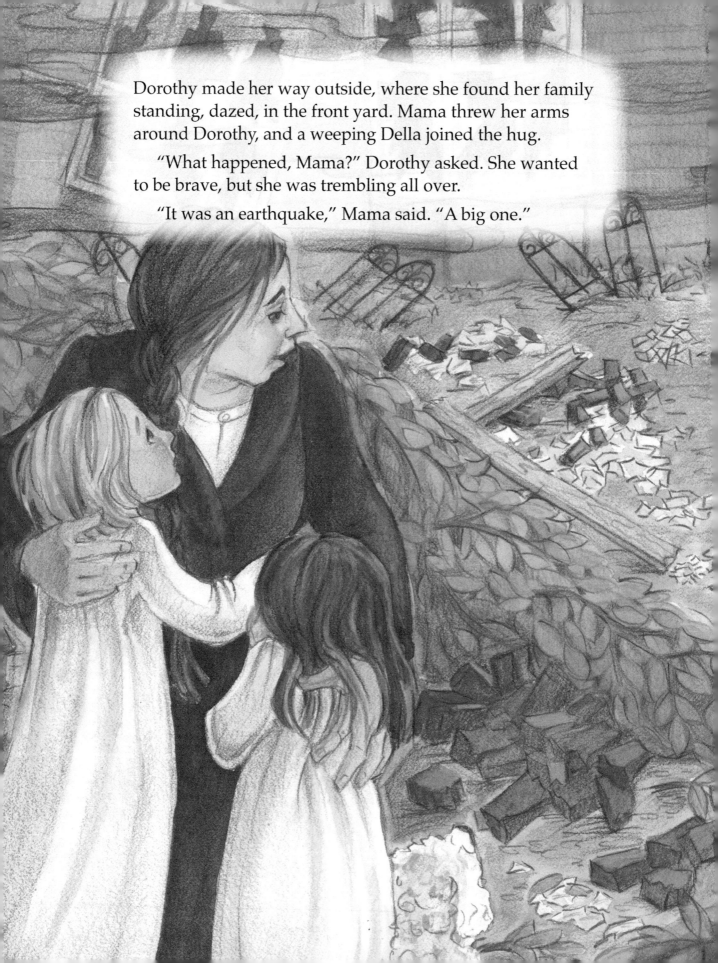

Dorothy made her way outside, where she found her family standing, dazed, in the front yard. Mama threw her arms around Dorothy, and a weeping Della joined the hug.

"What happened, Mama?" Dorothy asked. She wanted to be brave, but she was trembling all over.

"It was an earthquake," Mama said. "A big one."

All the neighbors were outside in their nightclothes. As dawn broke, they wandered about, staring at the damage. Chimneys had collapsed into big piles of bricks. Windows had shattered, spraying glass everywhere. Huge trees had toppled into the street, and the air was thick with dust. Papa and another man examined the crack that now ran from top to bottom through the Day home.

Every now and then, the earth would rumble and shake again, as if some underground giant were turning in his sleep.

Later that morning, Mama brought food
from inside the house, and they had
a strange picnic amid the uprooted trees.

Over the tops of the houses, the sky
turned darker and darker. At first,
Dorothy thought it was a storm; but
then she smelled smoke, and she saw the
bottoms of the "clouds" glowing orange.

"San Francisco is burning," Papa said.
"The fires are everywhere."

"Those poor people!" Mama exclaimed.

By evening, refugees began arriving—
a few at first, then hundreds of them,
fleeing the fires in San Francisco. By ferry
and by boat, they streamed across
the water into Oakland.

Weary from all their troubles, the strangers made a grim parade on their way past the Day home. One woman carried a baby, while two young children clutched at her skirt, crying that they were tired. None of them wore shoes.

Mama stepped toward the woman. "Come, now," she said. "Come rest with us. You must be exhausted."

She told Dorothy to fetch water, and Dorothy helped the little ones drink.

"My, you were thirsty!" she laughed after the little boy gulped down his third ladle of water.

Meanwhile, Papa dragged mattresses out of the house. All the neighbors were doing the same; no one wanted to sleep inside, in case there was another big shake. Mama began settling the exhausted refugees onto the mattresses. That left the Day family without beds to sleep on, but no one minded. The grass was soft, and they were all very tired.

First thing in the morning, Mama brought more food from the house to share with their guests. "These people don't have anything to eat," she explained to Papa. "We can't just let them go hungry!"

"But how can we feed so many?" Papa asked. Hundreds of people had settled in the neighborhood. "We don't have enough."

"Let's ask the neighbors to help!" suggested Donald.

Right away, Dorothy thought of Mrs. Reed's little grocery store, with its shelves full of food.

She ran to the store. Through the broken front window, she saw Mrs. Reed and Naomi cleaning up the huge mess the earthquake had made. All the shelves had toppled over, spilling jars and cans and boxes and apples and potatoes and onions everywhere. The Reeds looked tired and discouraged.

Dorothy hesitated, thinking of what the Reeds had said about her yesterday. What if Mrs. Reed didn't want to help a rough girl like her? For a moment, Dorothy felt angry again.

But in the next moment, the words flew from her mouth: "Can I help you?"

They looked up, startled. But Mrs. Reed was grateful. "That's very kind, Dorothy."

Naomi gave Dorothy a shy smile.

"We have to put the cans in crates," she explained. "We tried putting them back on the shelves, but the ground keeps shaking them off!"

That made both girls laugh.

"Mama is asking all the neighbors to help feed the people from San Francisco," Dorothy said as she stacked cans. "I think she wants to open her own restaurant, right on the front lawn!"

Naomi's eyes lit up. "Mama, we can help, can't we?"

Mrs. Reed considered the suggestion. "Yes, I think we could. In fact, I think we *should* supply Mrs. Day's outdoor eatery!"

Before long, they had loaded Mrs. Reed's red delivery cart with food, and Dorothy and Naomi set off, pulling it down the street together.

They found that Mama had set up her outdoor eatery in the park down the street, where the neighbors were putting up tents for all the refugees.

"Bring whatever you have for the soup," Mama told everyone she met. Papa and the boys had carried a big wood stove outside and started a fire in it, and Mama and some other women were heating large kettles of water.

Neighbors were bringing
vegetables for the soup, and
bread, too. Mrs. Reed came with
a surprise—two whole chickens
from the store's icebox.

"Why, thank you, Mrs. Reed,"
Mama said. She looked pleased.
"You have made this a real hearty
chicken soup!"

While the soup cooked, Mama put the girls to work collecting clothing. Dorothy, Della, and Naomi brought out clothes and shoes from the Day home, and before long the outdoor eatery was joined by a free clothing store.

Next, the girls organized games for the little children. They played hopscotch, jump rope, and Ring Around the Rosie. They read stories and sang songs.

Dorothy even comforted one crying child by letting the girl have Rebecca—
her favorite doll. Giving away Rebecca gave Dorothy a lump in her throat.
But all around her, people were giving away everything they had to help
the people from San Francisco. And Dorothy had never seen so many
smiles in the neighborhood, nor heard so much laughter.

And when the little girl hugged Rebecca, Dorothy smiled, too.

When the soup was ready to serve, Mama organized her helpers. "Dorothy, you can give out the bread," Mama said.

Dorothy couldn't help wondering whether there would be enough for everyone. There were only a few loaves of bread, and so many hungry people! But then Mr. Gerber brought three more loaves to share.

"It's a little stale, but the soup will soften it up, don't you think?" He winked at Dorothy and went off whistling.

He seemed happy, even though his store had been damaged by the "Great Quake," as people were calling the earthquake.

In fact, almost everybody seemed happy. Strangers smiled at one another, chatting and joking like old friends, their hearts warmed by charity and kindness.

Why can't it be this way all the time? Dorothy wondered.

And then she thought, maybe it *can* be this way . . . at least a little bit, at least some of the time.

"When I grow up, I'm going to have an outdoor eatery, just like this," Dorothy declared. "And an outdoor boarding house, too. All the beds will be on the lawn!"

Naomi laughed. "Can I get free desserts?" she asked.

"For sure!" Dorothy replied.

"Dorothy, I'm sorry for what I said yesterday," Naomi said. "I think my mother won't mind if we're friends again. Can we be?"

"Yes," Dorothy said, taking Naomi's hand.

"Soup's on!" announced one of the women helping Mama. A cheer went up from the crowd of hungry people, and Dorothy began handing out pieces of bread.

And, as it turned out, the bread didn't run out. Indeed, when everyone had eaten their fill, there was bread (and dessert) left over!

About Dorothy

Dorothy Day was born in Brooklyn, New York, on November 8, 1897. At the time of this story, she was eight years old; her sister, Della, was six; and she had two older brothers, ages eleven and ten. Later, her little brother was born. Her father was a newspaper sports reporter, and her mother took care of their home.

Dorothy and Della, 1910

Dorothy was a very spirited girl who loved nature, playing outdoors, imaginary games, reading, and writing little stories. She also had a temper that sometimes got her into trouble. She and Della were best friends all their lives, and she was always very close to her mother.

As a young woman, Dorothy was a journalist, writing articles for newspapers and magazines. She became more and more concerned about poor people. Always, she asked herself, "Why? Why can't the world be just and caring so that everyone can have enough?" She remembered how her mother and their neighbors came together to care for those in need after the 1906 San Francisco earthquake. Much later, she wrote about this in a book about her life, *The Long Loneliness*:

"I wanted everyone to be kind. I wanted every home to be open to the lame, the halt and the blind, the way it had been after the San Francisco earthquake. Only then did people really live, really love their brothers [and sisters]."

Dorothy's life changed in a wonderful way when she found out she was going to have a baby. She felt so grateful to God for this gift that she decided to have her little girl, Tamar, baptized, and then Dorothy herself became a Catholic in 1927. She prayed for a way to combine her new faith, her writing, and her love for the poor. God answered her prayers when she met Peter Maurin, who knew all about the Catholic Church's teachings on justice. Together they began the Catholic Worker Movement in 1933 in New York City. They started a newspaper, *The Catholic Worker*, to tell about the problems of the poor and working people, and what Christians should do to help them. They opened a soup kitchen for people with no jobs, and then houses of hospitality for homeless people. Hundreds joined them to do works of mercy and to protest injustice and war.

Dorothy became a great American leader in the struggle for justice and peace. She died on November 29, 1980. Her Catholic Worker Movement lives on today. About two hundred Catholic Worker houses serve people and advocate for peace and justice in fifteen countries.

Dorothy Day, 1952

Dorothy Day now has the title "Servant of God," which is the first step on the way to being named a saint in the Catholic Church.

The 1906 San Francisco Earthquake in Dorothy's Words

The earthquake that struck San Francisco at 5:12 a.m. on April 12, 1906, destroyed much of that city. The fires that followed drove many of its citizens to the nearby city of Oakland, which was affected by the earthquake but not the fires.

Dorothy wrote about her memories of the earthquake much later in a book called *From Union Square to Rome*:

"We were living in Oakland at the time and though I remember some years later praying fearfully during a lightning storm, I do not remember praying during that cataclysmic disturbance, the earthquake. And I remember it plainly. I was eight years old then. It was after two in the morning when it started, and it began with a fearful roaring down in the earth. It lasted for two minutes and twenty seconds, and there was plenty of time to have died of fright, yet I do not remember fear. It must have been either that I thought I was dreaming or that I was half conscious. Pictures fell from the walls, the bed rolled from one end of the polished floor to the other. My father got my brothers out of the house and my mother was able to carry my sister—God alone knew how she did it—out of the bungalow. I think the first shock was over before they got back to me.

"What I remember most plainly about the earthquake was the human warmth and kindliness of everyone afterward. For days refugees poured out of burning San Francisco and camped in Idora Park and the racetrack in Oakland. People came in their nightclothes; there were newborn babies.

"Mother had always complained before about how clannish California people were, how if you were from the East they snubbed you and were loathe to make friends. But after the earthquake everyone's heart was enlarged by Christian charity. All the hard crust of worldly reserve and prudence was shed. Each person was a little child in friendliness and warmth.

"Mother and all our neighbors were busy from morning to night cooking hot meals. They gave away every extra garment they possessed. They stripped themselves to the bone in giving, forgetful of the morrow. While the crisis lasted, people loved each other. They realized their own helplessness while nature 'travaileth and groaneth.' It was as though they were united in Christian solidarity. It makes one think of how people could, if they would, care for each other in time of stress, unjudgingly, with pity and with love."

Questions to Ponder

Following are the Corporal Works of Mercy found in the teachings of Jesus.

Feed the hungry

Give drink to the thirsty

Shelter the homeless

Clothe the naked

Visit the sick

Visit the imprisoned

Bury the dead

How many of the Works of Mercy can you find in *Dorothy and the Great Quake*?

What are some ways you and your family could do the Works of Mercy together in your home, neighborhood, church, or town?

Can you think of a miracle story in the Gospels that reminds you of what happened in this story? (Hint: It involves food!)

Look up what Jesus says about the Works of Mercy in the Bible (see Matthew 25:31–46). How can we do something kind and helpful for Jesus?

For more on Dorothy Day and
the Catholic Worker Movement,
see www.catholicworker.org.

Dorothy and the Great Quake: A Story about Dorothy Day as a Young Girl

Text copyright © 2019 by Barbara Allaire. All rights reserved.

Artwork copyright © 2019 by Vicki Shuck. All rights reserved.

Edited by Jerry Windley-Daoust.

Copy edited by Nancee Adams.

Proofread by Karen Carter.

Built by Steve Nagel.

The photos of Dorothy Day on pages 32-33 are courtesy of the Department of Special Collections and University Archives, Marquette University Libraries.

The quote on page 32 is from Dorothy Day, *The Long Loneliness: The Autobiography of Dorothy Day*, First Edition (New York: Harper & Brothers, Publishers), page 39.

The excerpt on page 33 is from Dorothy Day, *From Union Square to Rome*, First Edition (Silver Spring: Presentation of the Faith Press). Accessed at the Catholic Worker Movement website, www.catholicworker.org.

24 23 22 21 20 19   1 2 3 4 5 6 7 8 9

ISBN: 978-1-68192-535-6 (Inventory No. T2424)
LCCN: 2019942983

Our Sunday Visitor, Inc.
Huntington, Indiana
www.osv.com

Other OSV books for children:
Paddy and the Wolves: A Story about Saint Patrick as a Boy
The Little Flower: A Parable of St. Thérèse of Lisieux
Flowers for Jesus: A Story of Thérèse of Lisieux as a Young Girl
Molly McBride and the Purple Habit
Molly McBride and the Plaid Jumper
Molly McBride and the Party Invitation